DINO-SWIMMING

LISA WHEELER

ILLUSTRATIONS BY
BARRY GOTT

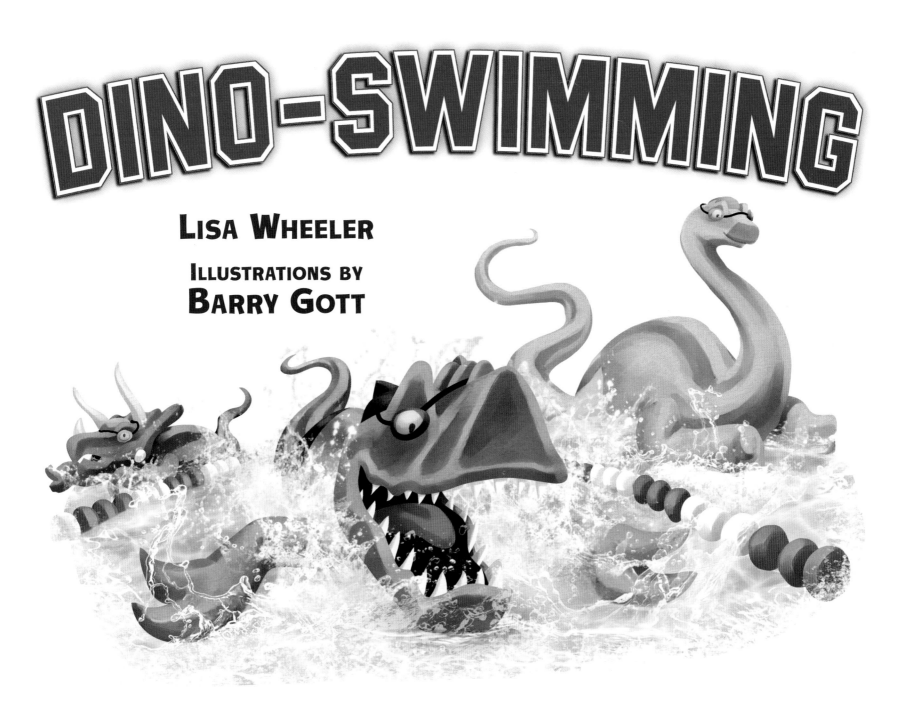

 CAROLRHODA BOOKS MINNEAPOLIS

To my mother-in-law, Carol Wheeler,
who taught my children to swim
—L.W.

For Rose, Finn, and Nandi
—B.G.

Carolrhoda Books
A division of Lerner Publishing Group, Inc.
241 First Avenue North
Minneapolis, MN 55401 USA

For reading levels and more information, look up this title at
www.lernerbooks.com.

Main body text set in Churchward Samoa Medium 24/36.
Typeface provided by Chank.

Library of Congress Cataloging-in-Publication Data

Wheeler, Lisa, 1963-
    Dino-swimming / by Lisa Wheeler ; illustrated by Barry Gott.
        p. cm.
    Summary: Plant-eating dinosaurs compete against meat-eating
dinosaurs at the swimming meet.
    ISBN 978-1-4677-0214-0 (lib. bdg. : alk. paper)
    [1. Stories in rhyme. 2. Dinosaurs—Fiction. 3. Swimming—Fiction.]
I. Gott, Barry, illustrator. II. Title
PZ8.3.W5668Dj 2015
    [E]—dc23   2013049181

Manufactured in the United States of America
1 - DP - 7/15/15

It's hot outside. Don't lose your cool.
Today's event is at the pool.

Come and watch two teams compete.
Hooray! A Dino-Swimming meet!

The **Land Sharks** show up dressed in red,
a fishy swim cap on each head.

Algae Eaters wear the green.
(Both the teams smell like chlorine.)

Goggles fit on dino eyes.
Trunks and suits are dino-size!

The lanes are ready. No delay.
"Let's get this swim meet under way!"

"We'll start off with a medley, folks!"
Each racer must swim all four strokes.

Up on the blocks, the dinos wait.
The buzzer sounds. Don't hesitate!

Butterfly up, backstroke back.
Raptor should outswim the pack.

Breaststroke third, and freestyle last.
    "It's Stegosaurus, moving fast!"
His strokes are smooth, without a flaw . . .
but **Raptor** wins it by a claw.

Stego pouts. He didn't win.

No time to sulk. It's time to swim!

Across the pool—a freestyle race.
Triceratops is in first place!

His goggles slip. He crosses lanes.

"Disqualified!"

He can't explain.

The other swimmers surge ahead.

Troodon wins it for the red!

5
6

LANE

1

PLACE

1:52.45

TIME

The Ptero Twins swim butterfly.
The Land Sharks' hopes are flying high.

There they go across the pool.
"It's a Pterodactyl duel!"

Those brothers brag and strut their stuff.
Till **T-Rex** tells them, "That's enough!"

Next up: no, not intermission.
It's the diving competition!

Divers prepare. Lane lines are moved.
Judges are ready. Dive list, approved.

Some swimmers dive, while others sit back.
They drink Dino-Ade and have a light snack.

When **Galli** is flipping through the air,
she has a certain style and flair.

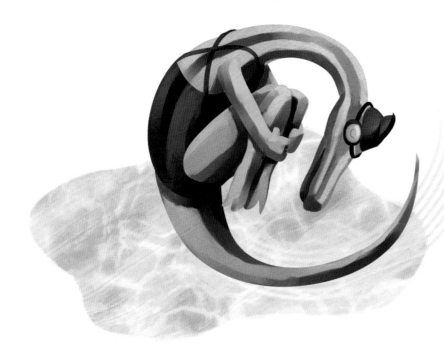

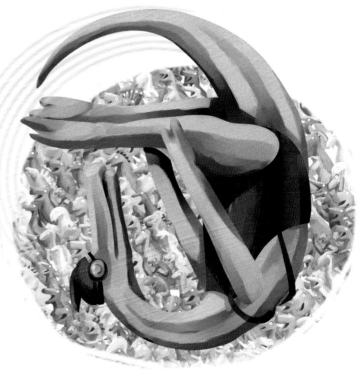

She tumbles and twists to *Ooohs* and *Ahhhs*.
Her entry is smooth. *Applause! Applause!*

Diplo's dive is not to be missed—
a somersault tuck with a neat little twist.

The twist is the part that's really cool.

SPLASH! Uh-oh!

He emptied the pool.

As **Diplo** gets reproved and grilled,
the swimming pool must be refilled.

Vendors venture through the stands,
raffle tickets in their hands.

"Come on, swim fans, try your luck!
"Support your team! Five for a buck!"

A newbie to the green-clad team,
Saurolophus is living her dream.

Backstroke is next—her nervous heart pounds.
She leaps before the buzzer sounds.

"False start!"
They must begin again.
Sauro wears an embarrassed grin.

The second start has no mistakes.
Sauro's head crest cuts the wakes.

Her trademark is a powerful kick.
Wide-webbed toes make this swimmer quick.

Thanks to those feet like walrus fins,
she pulls ahead . . . and Sauro wins!

Splashing, bobbing, water dripping,
Dino breaststroke, heads are dipping.

The Algae Eaters' hopes are heavy.
Ankylo's rhythm is slow and steady.

Allo's just behind the lead—
POW! That dino puts on speed!

Allosaurus takes the heat.
"The Land Sharks dominate the meet!"

Breaststroke's over. Relay time!
Dinos wait, four in a line.

Stego kicks with mighty feet.
Passes **Galli**. His flip turn is sweet!

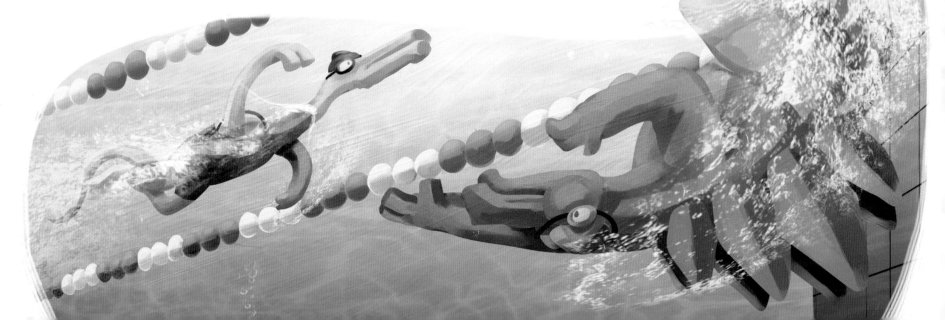

The green team swims out way ahead.
Looks like **Raptor's** ready for bed.

The **Land Shark** swimmers are really spent.
"The Algae Eaters take this event!"

At the end of the meet, the scoring's complete.
The **Land Sharks** win! The **Eaters** are beat!

The winners high-five in celebration.
The teams shake hands.
"Congratulations!"

Though swimming is over, these guys will be back . . .

. . . for **Dino-Racing** at the track!